Biscuit

story by ALYSSA SATIN CAPUCILLI

pictures by PAT SCHORIES

Sandy Creek

Sandy Creek
NEW YORK

An Imprint of Sterling Publishing
387 Park Avenue South
New York, NY 10016

Biscuit
Text copyright © 1996 by Alyssa Satin Capucilli
Illustrations copyright © 1996 by Pat Schories

This 2013 edition published by Sandy Creek by
arrangement with HarperCollins Publishers.

ISBN 978-1-4351-1709-9

Manufactured in Dong Guan City, China
Lot #:
14 15 16 17 SCP 10 9 8 7
01/14

This is Biscuit.

Biscuit is small.

Biscuit is yellow.

Time for bed, Biscuit!

Woof, woof!

Biscuit wants to play.

Time for bed, Biscuit!

Woof, woof!

Biscuit wants a snack.

Time for bed, Biscuit!

Woof, woof!

Biscuit wants a drink.

Time for bed, Biscuit!

Woof, woof!

Biscuit wants to hear a story.

Time for bed, Biscuit!

Woof, woof!

Biscuit wants his blanket.

Time for bed, Biscuit!

Woof, woof!

Biscuit wants his doll.

Time for bed, Biscuit!

Woof, woof!

Biscuit wants a hug.

Time for bed, Biscuit!

Woof, woof!

Biscuit wants a kiss.

Time for bed, Biscuit!

Woof, woof!

Biscuit wants a light on.

Woof!
Biscuit wants to be tucked in.

Woof!

Biscuit wants one more kiss.

Woof!

Biscuit wants one more hug.

Woof!

Biscuit wants to curl up.

23

Sleepy puppy.

Good night, Biscuit.

24